A Special Delivery To Die For

A Rockcrest Cove Mystery Series

Book 2

Emily Page

Table of Contents

Chapter One

The streets were slick from rain as Madeline maneuvered them with the finesse of a seasoned local. Her hands gripped the wheel a little tighter than usual and her feet held just enough tension as she prepared to apply the right amount of pressure to the brakes when needed to keep her from skidding across the slippery asphalt pavement.

The first rains of the year were always a little trickier to navigate than at any other time. Months of traffic during the dry months had left the roads with tiny droplets of oil and when mixed with the fresh rains created slippery patches slyly awaiting its first victim to send hydroplaning into another car like balls on a billiards table.

The red taillights of the car in front of her made her quickly tense up as she slammed on the brakes, hoping she wouldn't go careening into another direction she didn't want to go; the sudden change in speed made everything lunge forward. Instinctively, her right hand made that protective gesture to hold her packages in the passenger seat in place like a mother protecting a small child. She took her eyes off the road for a fraction of a second to make sure that her precious cargo was still safely in tact and to check the rearview mirror to make sure the car behind her was also able to stop.

A second later, the car ahead was moving again and she carefully moved her foot to the accelerator, moving forward once more, though slowly this time. Subconsciously, her hand moved a strand of lightly graying brown hair from in front of her eyes and she cursed slightly under her breath. Usually, she would be in deep meditation as she took to the roads, relishing in the freedom of time away from the bakery and a little solitude, but today traffic seemed a little more intense than usual.

Maybe it's me, she thought, *that is a little more tense than usual.* Her bakery had been doing quite well since that crazy fiasco with Emma Larson had finally been settled last year. The news of Emma's death had rocked the small town of Rockcrest Cove; it took quite a while for the incessant chatter to finally settle down and people to return to their tedious, mundane lives. Granted, it had been a very stressful time for Maddie; imagine being accused of something so heinous, but it also boosted her reputation in the eyes of the quaint little town. Her business excelled in ways she would have never imagined.

She turned the wheel and the car slipped quietly from the busy main thoroughfare to the quieter, more suburban streets of town.

This part of town was just a little more "posh" than where she lived and certainly had more class than the area where her bakery was located. You could tell that the cobblestone roadways were not used to a lot of traffic crossing them and the long and winding driveways that lead up to the grand estate houses harkened back to a gentler time than what Rockcrest Cove had seen lately.

Maddie glanced down at the paper taped to her dashboard and followed the directions carefully to the street she was looking for. *Right turn here, two blocks and then a left, then a quick right.* She leaned into the steering wheel as if the few extra inches would help her to see the street signs a little better. Three minutes later, she pulled into the driveway of a beautiful Victorian house, complete with the grand wraparound porch with rocking chairs set out on the veranda. Even in the rain, you can still smell the hint of paint in the air that told her that the white building with Kelly green trim had only recently been completed. The new residents were in the process of remodeling their home and were planning on being a part of this community for many more years.

The rain had eased up and was now a fine mist that made Maddie sit in the car for a minute. She took a quick glance in the mirror to check her hair and made a quiet sign of exasperation. She made an ineffectual attempt to pat down her mossy brown hair as though that was all it needed to keep the frizzies at bay. Another glance in the mirror told her that the attempt was futile, another ill side effect of the weather turning. The summer months were definitely over, and the next few months were going to be a struggle against the elements in every aspect of her life.

Opening the door just a crack in order to get her umbrella opened, she finally stepped out of the car and moved around to the passenger side door. Reaching in, she looked down at the floor and spoke to the canvas bag sitting there.

"Astoria, you need to stay here." She said. "I'll only be a minute."

A white ball of fur appeared at the top of the bag and then disappeared again into its cavernous regions again. Repositioning her handbag over her shoulder, she knelt down to pick up the three pink bakery boxes sitting on the seat and shut the door with her hip. A quick glance at the sky told her that a fresh downpour would be arriving any minute. Like a carefully practiced balancing act, she made her way to the veranda just before the downpour began.

Just before she reached the top step she felt that familiar tingle in her right hip and she was forced to set her packages down on the wrought iron table in order to grab her cell from her back pocket.

"Hello?"

"Hi Maddie, it's Rachel."

"Yes, Rachel." She answered as she cradled the phone in the crook of her neck and reached for the doorbell.

"I just had a quick question about the order for Tiffany?"

"Yes?"

"Did she want delivery today or was she supposed to come in for a pick up? There's no note on the order."

"Um, I think she wanted to pick them up." Maddie answered, unsure. "Her event won't be held at her house. Big secret thing, I guess."

"All right."

Maddie reached up to ring the doorbell a second time, but noticed the door was slightly ajar.

"Hmmm..." she voiced inquisitively.

"What's wrong?" Rachel asked into the phone.

Strange, Maddie said to herself. "I'm at the Stevens' house to make the delivery and there's no answer at the door."

"Maybe she's around back," Rachel said into the phone. "It's a big house."

"Perhaps," Maddie agreed. "Don't hang up," she cautioned, "I want to check it out."

"Hello?" she called out, quickly setting her cell to snap pictures and immediately took a picture of the front door ajar as she had found it. She called into the room again. "Hello?" The house had an empty quality that echoed back to her that there was no one home. "Is anybody here?" she tried again, but still there was no response.

She reached out and gave the door a tentative push and watched as it opened wider. "Hang on the phone a minute," she said to Rachel. "Something doesn't feel right here."

"Really?" Rachel asked.

Gingerly, she picked up her packages off the table and stepped over the threshold into the cavernous entrance of the house. The foyer was a plain affair with a handy coat rack in one corner and a hat and umbrella stand in the other. Next to the stand was a small wooden bench, she assumed was used for people putting on their footwear before heading out the door. The room had that exotic Asian feeling with an ample supply of house slippers next to the shoe rack.

"Um, I'm Maddie from the Cake's Cradle with your delivery..."she said in a sing-songy voice.

The silence in the house gave her the impression that it had been empty for quite some time. There was no sound from the upstairs or the back. She stood there in the foyer for just a moment while she contemplated whether or not to go further into the house. She thought about calling the police, but they weren't going to come just because some silly old lady thought something was wrong.

She could only see from the foyer into the spacious living room where the Stevens more than likely entertained and welcomed a long parade of guests. Since it was possible to see only partly into the room, Maddie took a tentative step forward into the large expanse and immediately turned up her nose at the nouveau riche décor. *Clearly*, she thought to herself, *here was someone who was quite proud to flaunt her money and show off her success.* It was finely decorated with an odd mixture that told of Ana's many travels around the world. The east-meets-west motif didn't quite come off too well with odd combinations of wall hangings from around the world, sofa pillows from India, or maybe it was Indonesia, rugs from somewhere in the Middle East, and tall, thin, African wood carvings to finish it off. On the mantle was a clutter of pictures of Ana in front of the pyramids of Egypt, the Great Wall of China, and even one at the Berlin Wall before it came crashing down.

On the far side of the room between the living room and the dining room was a landing with a staircase that led to the more private upstairs living area. The lower half of the staircase led down into the dining area opposite the main entrance to the living room.

"Rachel, you still there?" she whispered into the phone as she walked past the staircase into the dining room.

"Yes, ma'am. Still here."

"Ok, don't hang up, whatever you do. I may need you to call the police, but wait until I say so."

"All right."

Maddie wrinkled up her nose again; it was nice stuff, but it seemed to be a bit of overkill. She called out again; she just wanted to get her delivery done and be on her way.

"Rachel, are you still there?"

"Yes, I'm here," came the reply.

"Are you sure the order was for a delivery today?"

"Yes, ma'am," she confirmed. "They said they had to have it by early afternoon."

"Well, I'm here and there's not a soul around," Maddie reiterated. "The door was open," she said and then corrected. "Well, it was not really pulled closed is more like it."

"Maybe they had some sort of emergency and had to leave in a hurry."

"Yes, that would explain the door not being completely closed," Maddie agreed as she made her way into the dining room where she left her packages on the table before heading into the kitchen. "Oh my God," Maddie said. "Something is very wrong here."

The room was not quite in complete disarray, but Maddie got the sense that something awful had happened there. The table was set for two, but food was still on the plates from the night before, partially eaten. Utensils were strewn across the floor and a lone wine glass with its contents splattered across the hardwood floor, the stain already set in stone. On the other side of the table was a stack of papers seemingly untouched by the chaos that occurred on the other side of the room.

"Rachel!" Maddie said into the phone. "I think something happened here."

"Oh my gosh, Ms. Maddie. Are you sure?" Rachel gasped into the phone.

Maddie's eyes surveyed the room observing all of the little details. She started snapping pictures of everything she saw. A stack of business papers strewn across the dining room table and a few on the floor, two plates of food half eaten, and a broken wine glass, its contents splayed across the floor. "Mmm hmm," She said as she snapped another picture. "Pretty sure."

She walked further into the spacious kitchen before turning back towards the way she came when she noticed something on the landing of the staircase leading upstairs.

"There's something on the stairs," she said, taking it upon herself to investigate.

As Maddie walked over, she suddenly stopped short. A lone foot, wearing a stylish stiletto, could be seen on the bottom step above the landing. As she rounded the corner, she could see the owner of the shoe.

"Oh my God!" Maddie exclaimed as she hurried over to the woman lying at the bottom of the last riser, a pool of dried blood surrounding her head like a halo. "She's dead."

"What!" Rachel wanted to confirm.

"Yes, I'm sure...but," she hesitated for a moment. "You need to phone the police right away." She paused for a second to slow down the rapid beating of her heart. "Don't hang up the phone, dear. Stay on the line with me until they come. You know how difficult Chief Conner's can be."

"Yes, ma'am. I do," Rachel put down the phone and used the other extension to dial 911.

Maddie could hear her through the line as she made her way back through the house to the front door. Suddenly, she remembered Astoria was still sitting in the car. She walked out the door and rushed over to her own car to let Astoria out to walk about the yard and stretch her legs while Maddie waited for the police.

Deciding not to reenter the house, she started to investigate the estate's surroundings. There was a path leading around the side of the house to a beautifully manicured Japanese garden. The stone walkway was well manicured, but even after this morning's rain, muddy footprints could be seen at the end of the path that lead to a small, seemingly unoccupied gardener's cottage. She looked closely at the tiny building that stood in stark contrast to the impressive house that she had just left. With several panes broken out and the last vestiges of paint barely visible to the naked eye, the color had faded from the effects of the constantly changing climate to the tiny flecks of hue that seemed to desperately try to hang on to what remained of the small cabin.

Astoria began to stroll down the garden path leading away from the house compelling Maddie to pick her up. Noticing the muddy footprints leading away from the house, she didn't want her cat to disturb the scene in case it was possibly connected to what had happened.

The path lead to a small patch of earth that seemed to have been the only area of land that was not carefully manicured to give that exotic Japanese garden type feel. The square patch looked as if it were being prepared for something special.

Putting Astoria back into her canvas bag, she went back to the safety of the veranda and looked back towards the path. Taking out her camera, she zoomed in to get a few shots of the path, the cottage, and what was left of the footprints leading away from the house.

Even if it turned out not to be evidence, the pictures would tell a very nice story.

Maddie had thought to investigate further, but the wail of the police sirens in the distance told her that she should turn back to meet them when they arrived.

Chapter Two

Three black and whites appeared in rapid succession on the drive leading up to the house. They rounded the curve of the driveway and came careening to a slippery halt on the wet pavement in front. Immediately, a host of officers descended upon the scene with their arms at the ready position, fingertips only inches from their holstered weapons.

Chief Connors lifted his mighty bulk from his vehicle with only a little amount of effort. *My gosh,* Maddie thought, *he looks even bigger than I remembered.* A bitter taste formed in her mouth as she remembered her first encounter with the man and those old feelings started to rise again. She had to force herself to put the past completely out of her mind once again and focus on the poor dead woman she had found presently.

She took a few steps towards the chief who had finally pulled himself up to his full stature and stood gazing about. Maddie approached and as the two made eye contact she could see the recognition fly across his face. *Yes,* she thought to herself, *he remembers her, too.*

"Chief," Maddie approached, extending her hand in a businesslike fashion.

"Mrs. McDougal," he responded without returning the gesture.

Clearly, there were hard feelings that were still festering like open wounds from that fateful day last year.

Connors appeared to be biting the inside of his lip. "Didn't expect to find you here."

"Didn't Rachel tell you?" Maddie inquired.

"Rachel," Connors said. "Who's that?"

"She's the one who made the call." Connors looked perplexed, but didn't say anything. "I was on the phone with her when I found the body. I told her to make the call."

Connors just stared at Maddie, his face showing a myriad of expressions. It appeared that he choose not to say the words that were obviously fighting their way to the surface and instead turned to one of his deputies to start barking instructions. He turned away from Maddie without another word.

She stood and observed the busywork of the officers before opening her car door to let Astoria, who had been rubbing against her leg, back into the car. She paid little attention to her constant companion and gave her an absentminded pat on the head before shutting her car door once again.

Back in the dining room, she found Connors and three other deputies stooped over Ana's body, examining the details of the surroundings. Already, one deputy was busy pulling out the yellow crime scene tape she had become all too familiar with. Ana's shoe, lying on the stairs in her home, gave the appearance that she had fallen down the steps on her way down to the kitchen. *Perhaps the thin heels and extra height had not given her the grace she had hoped for. After all, isn't that why we wear stilettos, to look more leggy and graceful?* Maddie thought to herself once again.

Connors stood up from the scene and his eyes quickly canvassed the room. He saw everything that Maddie had seen and she was sure that he would recognize that something was amiss in the picture.

"Looks pretty obvious to me," Connors spoke. "An apparent accident." He said. "Looks like she maybe missed a step or stumbled as she was coming down the stairs, fell, and hit her head." He shook his head sadly from side to side. "Sad story, this one."

"An accident?" Maddie looked appalled. "Is that all you plan to say?"

Connors pulled his body back into a full standing position before he turned to face his nemesis.

"Yes," he said. "It should be pretty obvious what happened here. Even for you," he added, a note of derision in his voice.

"Yes, I admit it appears that way," she gestured towards the spilled wine on the dining room floor, the extra place setting at the table, and the scattered papers. "Obviously, she was not here alone. Someone was with her and there was a struggle." She pointed at the untouched food. "Look, they didn't even finish their meal." Frustrated, she pointed to the open back door. "Someone went out the back door in a hurry!" she exclaimed getting a little excited. "There's even footprints on the garden path!"

Connors' eyes carefully followed Maddie's finger as she pointed out all the evidence in front of them. His face made a poor attempt at hiding his contempt for this woman, but it was clear she was going to be just as insistent as she was the last time they bumped heads. "Well, there could have been quite a few reasons for these things. It's not our business to investigate the personal affairs of the lives of every person who dies here in Rockcrest Cove."

"I'm not expecting you to speak on the personal affairs of everyone here in town, but clearly there is more to what happened here than what you're concluding. This bears an investigation."

Connors raised his hand and beckoned for one of his deputies to come. "Thank you Mrs. McDougal. Perhaps you can give your statement to officer Fellows here."

Maddie couldn't believe her ears. He was going to brush off this case as well. Flabbergasted, she stood rooted in place when the officer tried to redirect her away.

"But..." she tried to interject, but Connors was already moving away from her and talking to another officer about the case. "Chief Connors," she called. "Connors!" she called again.

Connors showed no sign that he had heard her, although she knew he did.

~~~

The hour before the bakery closed was one of the busiest Maddie had ever seen. The Friday before

Veterans Day, the last holiday before the winter season set in, was always busy, but this day seemed to be more than usual. Maddie thought about it and tried to figure out why; she finally conceded that it might not have been as busy as it seemed. It could very well be her frustration at the realization that Chief Connors was about to bungle another important investigation.

Admittedly, she was still brooding over his mistreatment of her with the Emma Larson case, but this time she was convinced that Ana's death was no accident; something was terribly wrong and the frustration inside her was mounting.

Finally, the last customer left her store and she was free to relax for a minute. Exhausted, she sat down in her office chair and wiped the sweat from her brow with her forearm; a strand of grayish brown hair fell from her tousled mop and hung there just to the side of her line of vision. She mused over her dilemma for a little bit longer before she picked up the phone and dialed.

"Hey Gran," Bailey's voice came on the line.

"Hey darling," Maddie said. "Listen, are you busy right now?"

"No Gran. What's up?"

"I wonder if you could come by the store for a bit. Something has happened and I could use your assistance."

"Sure, Gran. What is it?" Bailey asked inquisitively.

"I'd rather tell you when you get here," Maddie said.

"All right," she agreed, her tone a little higher than usual, her curiosity peaked. "Can you give me 15 minutes?"

"Sure. I'll be waiting for you in the office. Oh, and by the way, can you stop by and pick up Eleanor on the way?"

"Sure thing, Gran."

"I'll call her and tell her you're coming."

They said their goodbyes and hung up the phone. Maddie quickly dialed Eleanor's number and made the same invitation. She knew that both women were perplexed about the nature of her call, but it was just something she didn't want to do over the phone or have to repeat over and over again. With both of them there, she could put it all out in the open and be done with it. She didn't look forward to having to tangle with Connors again, and certainly not so soon after the Emma Larson case.

Maddie took out her notes she had made from her observations at the Stevens' home and started to peruse them. Maybe it was nothing, but she felt it was at least worth checking out. It had been nagging at her all day and she couldn't get it out of her mind. She had to do something to make sure that Ana's death was not going to be simply swept under the rug.

As promised, Bailey and Eleanor arrived at the bakery just as Maddie had requested. Bailey was looking her usual perky self wearing a casual pair of jeans, a light jacket, and toting her designer umbrella that was large enough to cover all three women if needed. Eleanor on the other hand, a professor at the local college, was still dressed in her daytime professional attire. Wearing a tailored jacket, fashionable, yet expensive, black pumps, and swinging a matching handbag, she was poised and ready to take on whatever challenge she knew her childhood friend had in store. Unlike Bailey, Eleanor was never surprised when Maddie called and had pretty much surmised that they were going to be thick in the soup of something very soon. She pulled her iPad out of her bag and was ready to record anything she found to be of importance.

Maddie quickly ushered the two women into the back office and put the closed sign in place so that no one else would be tempted to stop by if they saw any signs of life. The store had been so busy lately that some people didn't even look at the sign. If they noticed people inside they would expect to be served. Turning off the lights in the front of the store, she instructed her staff to finish the closing routine without her as she hurried to the back room to chat with her visitors.

"Thank you both for coming so quickly," Maddie said as she entered the room and shut the door. "I just wanted to run something by the two of you if you don't mind."

Bailey had a concerned look on her face. "Sure, Gran. What's wrong?"

"Well, it has nothing to do with me, but I am concerned," Maddie started to explain to ease Bailey's rising fears. She paused and took a deep breath before continuing. "It seems that there's been another murder."

"What!?" Bailey exclaimed. "Who? Where?" She started looking around the room as if she would still be able to find the body lying in plain view.

"Calm down, Bailey," Maddie said quietly. "It wasn't here, this time, and it has absolutely nothing to do with me."

Bailey visibly began to relax and settle down. She was still a little gun shy after the murder last year. She wasn't so sure she could go through all of that again.

"Who's the victim?" Eleanor spoke up for the first time.

"Ana Stevens," Maddie offered. "I stumbled across the body this morning when I went to make a delivery for an order she placed last week."

"You found the body?" Bailey interrupted. "Is Chief Connors going to try to blame you for this murder, too?"

Maddie gave her a patronizing smile. "Not this time dear. That's the problem."

"What do you mean?" Eleanor asked confused.

"Well, it seems that Chief Connors is not entirely convinced that there was a murder after all." She took another breath. "Apparently, he's convinced it was an accident."

"Hmmm," Eleanor said in deep thought. "What makes you think he's wrong?" she asked, taking on the role of Switzerland. As a professor of criminal justice, she was in the habit of gathering all of her facts together before she made any type of comment.

Maddie reached in her hip pocket and pulled out her phone where she had discreetly taken a few photos of the crime scene before the police had unceremoniously removed her from the premises. She handed the phone to the women as her decree of proof.

The two women leaned over the small screen to try to see what Maddie had been trying to capture.

"I can't see anything on there. It's too small," Bailey complained. "Let me do something real quick." She reached into her large bag and pulled out a few cords and walked over to where Maddie was sitting behind her desk. "May I?"

"By all means," Maddie said and relinquished her chair to Bailey.

The two women watched her connect Maddie's phone to her computer and deftly download the photos on the screen and then send the photos to the printer where they had hard copies of the crime scene in less than 5 minutes. With the pictures spread out before them, the three women were able to look more closely at the images and see every single detail.

"My Maddie," Eleanor exclaimed. "You did a nice job of getting all the details of the scene for us." She turned up her nose and scrutinized one little part of the picture. "What's this?" she said pointing a finger at a small object on the table in one of the pictures.

Maddie looked closely at the object and scrunched up her nose as well. "I don't really know. I don't remember seeing it when I was there."

Bailey leaned in and looked at it as well. "It kinda looks like an earring," she concluded. "See the pokey thingy part that goes through the ear? It's right there."

"Yeah, you're right, but what's that symbol on it?"

The three women scrutinized the photo, but none of them recognized it.

"I'd say we have our first clue," Eleanor announced. "But before we start investigating this thing, we need to get a little more information about Ana.

We need to rule out all possibilities. So we must to first rule out Chief Connors' belief that it was an accident."

Maddie looked up at her friend. "But Eleanor, don't you see here that it is obvious that there was an altercation right there in the kitchen?"

"It certainly appears that way, but we have to be absolutely sure," Eleanor pointed out. "Having a disagreement doesn't necessarily translate into murder. If that were the case, we would all be dead. We have to be sure," she continued. "Why, we don't even know if anyone would have reason to want her dead. We first have to determine a motive for killing her and then find someone who actually had the opportunity to make it happen."

The women all agreed that Eleanor was right. While Maddie was the quick, shoot-from-the-hip type, Eleanor had a more practical approach to the same problem. They first needed to determine a motive.

"Ok," Eleanor took the lead, "what do we know about Ana?"

They were all silent for a moment. They really didn't know too much about her. She traveled in a completely different circle from them.

"I know she runs that fancy, shmansy travel agency that plans those exotic around the world trips," Bailey offered.

"Yeah," Maddie chimed in, "I've read about those trips. I've always wanted to go on one, but it is well out of my price tag."

"Mine too," Eleanor agreed. "But, I do know that I've heard of several cases where her customers weren't entirely satisfied with their trip and have sued her for their money back. She charges a pretty penny for those big affairs, you know."

"Maybe one of her dissatisfied customers could be behind all of this?" Maddie proposed out loud.

"Perhaps, but we need to find out about her business. There seems to be a lot of business papers thrown about the room," Eleanor said, examining one of the photos.

"I guess the best place to start is to visit her office," Bailey suggested. "It's just, I don't think we can walk in and start asking questions and they'll answer us just like that."

"Maybe not," Maddie said. "Maybe we can come up with a good cover story."

Astoria, her Persian cat, was scratching at the door wanting to come in from roaming about outside the back door of the store. Maddie always let her out for a little while after closing.

"What kind of cover story could we come up with? It's not like we're pros at this," Bailey wondered.

"Well, we'll think of something," Maddie encouraged as she kicked off her working shoes and reached for her street shoes. "I mean all sorts of businesses must book trips through travel agencies, right?"

"You're saying that we should go in and pretend like we're going to book a trip to ah, to ah, ..." Bailey was snapping her fingers as if it would make her mind work better.

"To a baker's convention!" Maddie said excitedly. She started shuffling the papers around on her desk. "There's one coming up soon. I got the announcement in the mail the other day." She started rummaging through the paperwork on her desk. "I know it's here somewhere. They're going to be announcing a new line of appliances for professional bakers."

Her attention was divided between the mountain of work on her desk and Astoria clawing at her feet.

"Not now, Astoria," She said irritated. "Not now." She gave the cat a gentle kick. Astoria sauntered away, but was back again, playfully swatting at her shoe.

"Let me see," Maddie said, thinking out loud again. "I know I put it here somewhere." Again she gave her cat a gentle nudge. "Astoria," she said, slightly irritated, "what is it?" To Bailey and Eleanor she apologetically stated, "She's not usually like this. I don't know what's gotten into her today."

"I do," Eleanor said pointing at Maddie's shoe, "there's something stuck to the bottom of your shoe."

Maddie stopped what she was doing and slipped off her shoe. She flipped it over to examine the bottom and found a small earring stuck to it. She pulled it out to examine it more closely.

"I think that's the thing we saw in the photo," Bailey said reaching for it. "Yes, I'm sure of it." She grabbed the printed photo and put them next to one another. "Look!" She laid the earring down on top of the photo so that they could all see.

"You must have stepped on it when you were at the Stevens' house."

"Yeah. I guess so."

"This is definitely our first clue," Eleanor said. "At least we've confirmed that someone was with Ana the night she died and it must've been a woman."

"NO!" shouted Bailey. "Men wear earrings, too!"

Chapter Three

At first glance, the Stevens Travel Agency seemed no different than any other. As you entered the front door, the typical wide-open reception room was similar to other agencies; four desks, one in each corner where the travel agents worked booking typical airline flights, cruises, and other travel packages for the average traveler and big posters on the walls boasting getaways to tropical resorts and fantasy packages for the most popular destinations around the world. It was exactly what you'd expect from a travel service.

Maddie and Bailey made a point to stand out from the typical traveler. Maddie had put on her one and only charcoal black designer dress and her most expensive pair of shoes, hoping they didn't recognize that she was five years out-of-date. Bailey wore designer jeans with stylish camel-colored stilettos, a navy blue silk polka-dotted blouse, and camel-colored sweater layered on top; she pulled her long hair back taut into a ponytail. Whether they were able to pull off their "woman of substance" appearance they were unsure, but soon after they entered the office, a woman appeared through a side door greeting them with an extended hand.

"Hello," she said, giving Maddie a soft handshake. "My name is Jessica, how can I be of assistance?"

"My name is Madeline McDougal and this is my granddaughter, Bailey. We were looking for a European tour package, but we just couldn't bear one of those traditional package tours with a bunch of people from who-knows-where traveling with us. But we've often heard that Stevens has some awesome travel deals that would be worth looking into."

"Why, of course," Jessica replied. "I'd be happy to assist you with anything you need."

"Well, we were hoping to see Ana. That's who we were told to ask for."

Jessica looked a little taken aback for only a half a beat. "Well, I'm afraid that's not possible," she finally said. "Perhaps you would like to speak with her assistant, Thomas. He'll be stepping in and filling Ana's shoes now."

"Yes, we'd like that," Maddie said.

Jessica quickly ushered the two women through the two elaborate side doors into a much more stylish office. Cherry wood paneling lined the walls with vast windows that overlooked the park across the street. They were seated in front of a massive wooden desk that Maddie thought would be much better suited for a corporate affair than for a travel agency. It appeared that Ms. Ana Stevens loved to live well beyond her means.

"Thomas will be with you shortly."

"Thank you," The two women said and Jessica politely excused herself.

As soon as she had left the room, Maddie and Bailey looked at each other in amazement.

"Wow! This was a travel agency?" Bailey exclaimed. "Oh-my-God!" she said, stressing every word. "This lady really liked to put on the dog!"

"You think *this* is special, you should see her house," Maddie added.

"No!" Bailey looked at her grandmother. "You've got to be kidding me!"

"No. Not at all." Maddie said. "Her home is far more elaborate than this."

Bailey looked nonplussed. "Gran, I think we're in the wrong business."

Maddie gave her granddaughter a slight little chuckle, but said nothing in return.

~~~

Thomas entered the room with a cacophony of noise. He was definitely not what either of the ladies expected to see. He wore a pair of pinstriped jeans that were just a tad too tight and a sports jacket that looked like it was left over from the 80s. His hair was slicked back with enough oil to lubricate his car and he walked with a slight swagger that made people wonder about him.

"Yes, ladies. My name is Thomas. I understand you're looking to see Ana today."

"Yes, that's right," Maddie said.

"Well, I'm sorry to be the bearer of bad news," he said with his hand waving at nothing, "but Ana met with an unfortunate accident yesterday." He made a pretense of being disheartened. "She's no longer with us."

"What happened?" Bailey asked, trying to appear interested.

"Apparently, she had a slip and fall and hit her head on the stairs." He made a rather insincere attempt at a sigh. "The police said she'd probably been drinking and lost her balance." He gestured towards two chairs sitting across from the desk that seemed far too large for the space that held it. You could tell that he wanted to say more, but he pulled himself in check and reined in whatever thought he was about to reveal.

"I'm sorry," Maddie said. "I didn't have the pleasure of meeting her in person, so I don't know her at all."

"Oh my goodness!" Thomas exclaimed. "I didn't realize...I just assumed that you knew her."

"No. I was to meet her yesterday when I went to her home. She had placed a large order from my bakery for a special event she was planning that was supposed to have happened yesterday."

A look of confusion spread across Thomas' face and he stood just staring at the two women for a minute. "I'm sorry," he asked perplexed, "why are you here?" The confusion quickly was evolving into a look of suspicion.

"No, Thomas," Maddie said, "it is we who should apologize." She looked across the big desk at what she saw was a confused little boy. "Let me explain. You see, I was the one that found Ana's body yesterday when I went to make the delivery at her house."

Thomas' hand went up to his throat. "Oh my God! You poor dear!" Then he leaned his chest across the desk. "Was it awful? Horrible? I just don't know what I would have done if it had been *me*."

Maddie gave him a puzzling look and eyed the young man suspiciously. He certainly didn't seem like he was distraught in the least.

"Well, yes, it was quite horrible to say the least," Maddie ventured. "I just didn't know what to do. Of course, I phoned the police right away, but I was just hoping that I could find out more about Ana if I came into the office."

"My goodness, I can just imagine what a shock it was for you. Would you like me to order you some tea or anything?" Thomas offered.

"No, I'm fine," Maddie assured him. "I was just wondering how everything was getting along, you know, notifying the family that sort of thing."

"Well, Ana didn't have much family to speak of. She was divorced and alone as far as I knew."

"Really? That must have been so sad. I thought I could send my condolences to the family."

"Well, I'm sorry to tell you, but Ana didn't have any family that we knew about, but she had quite a few friends that may be saddened by the loss."

Maddie looked appraisingly at the young man. She couldn't quite figure him out just yet. This little side trip was proving far more interesting than she had ever imagined. She remained silent for a minute, not sure what exactly to say to this strange little man sitting in front of her. She quickly took a side-glance at Bailey for some help, but found that she was even more confounded by Thomas.

She hesitated before she ventured to say anything more. "Let me ask you, Thomas." She paused to make sure she had his full attention. "Can you think of anyone that might want to see Ana dead?"

Thomas sat back in his seat and eyed the two ladies for only a half a second. It appeared as if he was trying to decide if he should continue to talk to them. Finally, he spoke up, "Well, I'll tell you this much. Ana was a pretty determined businesswoman. And because of that she did ruffle a few feathers. For that she had a number of people who certainly weren't happy with the way she did business."

"Really?" Bailey had finally come out of her stunned silence.

"Yes. As a matter of fact, there were quite a few unhappy customers in here on a regular basis." He paused for a second before continuing in a more hushed tone. "If you ask me, I wouldn't be surprised if someone didn't want to see her gone."

"Do you really think it was that many people?" Maddie asked.

"Well, I've been working for Ana for several years. Her business ethics weren't always above board. There were quite a few accusations about her using customer's money to pay for her personal expenses. I can tell you this because it's already public knowledge. You can go online and find out much of this for yourself," he sighed in exasperation. "Customers come to use for the best in exclusive vacations, and they would pay thousands of dollars for that exclusivity. They claimed that Ana would take their money and then give them a cheaper vacation package and pocket the difference. Most of the time, people didn't notice it, but those that did, weren't very happy."

This time it was Maddie who leaned across the desk. "You wouldn't happen to have a list of those customers would you?"

Thomas rose from his seat and walked across the room to a single file cabinet. "Here it is," he said as he tapped his finger on the lone cabinet sitting in the corner.

"You mean the file is in there?" Bailey asked.

"No, I mean this *is* the file. Ana has had this business for many years. That's a long time to collect rivals and enemies."

"The whole drawer?" Bailey asked again trying to clarify.

"It's the whole cabinet. It goes back more than 10 years. Long before I started working here." He walked back to his desk and sat down with an exhaustive sigh.

Maddie eyed the cabinet and wondered if it would be safe to ask to look at some of the files. *Nothing ventured, nothing gained,* she thought. "Do you think I could get a peak at some of those files?"

Thomas again got that indecisive look on his face as if he was trying to decide if he should say or provide any more information. "Well, in my opinion, it will take a long time to pick through all of those files and I'm not sure what you're looking for anyway." A broad smile crossed his face, " But I have a better idea."

"Oh really? What?"

"Well, next week we're having a Paddlewheel River Cruise to remember Ana. We thought that it could be sort of a blanket apology and a way to make amends for all the things she's been accused of. At least that's the plan."

"Oh really? I think that's a great idea."

"My bet is that if someone really wanted her dead, they'll be on that boat with us."

"That's perfect!" Bailey exclaimed. "Is it possible for us to get on the cruise too?"

"It's possible, if the cruise actually happens. For some reason the Chief of Police, Connors I think is his name, wants to approve it first."

Hmmm, Maddie thought. *Maybe he is taking this investigation more seriously than she thought.* "Well, if it's approved, will you let us know?"

"Sure, thing," Thomas agreed. "Just make sure you leave your information with Jessica before you leave." He reached over and hit the intercom.

"And Thomas, you've been so helpful to us today, I hate to ask one more favor."

"It's not a problem. What can I do for you?"

"Could you try to come up with a list of some of her possible enemies or rivals before the cruise for us?" She gave him a genuine smile before she continued, "I know this is not an official investigation, but we'd really like your input."

Thomas' eyes beamed with pride. "Of course, I'd be happy to. I'll make sure you get it before the cruise so you have plenty of time to look it over. I'll even put in my opinions on who I think might have done it."

A second later Jessica came into the room.

"Jessica, these ladies would like to book passage on the Paddleboat Cruise, can you get their information and make sure they're taken care of?"

"Sure thing," she said, looking at the women strangely.

"If you'll excuse me," Thomas said, "I'm already late for an appointment. We'll have to catch up on our discussion on the cruise if that's all right with you."

"Of course," Maddie agreed. "It was a pleasure to meet with you, Thomas."

"It was a pleasure to meet with you, too," he said, and then he was gone.

Jessica moved over behind the desk and lit up the computer screen.

"May I have your names please?"

"Madeline McDougal."

"Magdeline MacDougal," Jessica repeated.

"No, Madeline. McDougal."

"Isn't that what I said?" she asked perplexed.

"No, you said Magdeline MacDougal. It's Madeline."

"Can you spell it for me please?"

"Yes. It's M-A-D-E-L-I-N-E."

"Oh, Madeline," she repeated as she typed away at the keyboard. "And the last name?"

"Capital M-C," Madeline waited to make sure that she got that right before she went on with the rest of the name. "Dougal, D-O-U-G-A-L."

"Madeline McDougal. Got it." She turned her attention to Bailey next, "And your name?"

"Guest." Bailey was not about to go through a spelling fiasco with this nutcase. "Just put me down as her guest."

"All right. I look forward to seeing you both there."

"Oh, you're planning to come, too?"

"Yes, several of us from the office will be there."

"Great, we'll see you then."

Chapter Four

They arrived at the Paddleboat a little before six in the evening with their tickets in hand. They were told it would be a very casual affair and there was no need to dress up for the occasion. Maddie wasn't really sure how extreme the event would be, but expected with all those who had a grudge against Ana, she should be ready for just about anything.

Bailey, on the other hand, came packing. She wasn't about to take any chances with so many possible irate people on board. She had a small Kimbler Ultra CDP II in her handbag. She knew her Gran's potential for getting into trouble and she was determined to be ready for whatever may happen on the cruise. She didn't tell her Gran she was carrying a gun because she knew she wouldn't approve, but nevertheless, they were planning on finding a murderer, which meant anything could happen.

As they crossed the ramp and boarded the Paddleboat, they were utterly surprised at the number of people present. Thomas gave them sufficient enough warning that they would have their hands full sifting through possible suspects, but they certainly weren't expecting to see so many people with a grudge against Ana. The two women stood at the entrance to the dining room and observed the quiet remembrance of the woman's demise. Of course, no one was speaking openly about his or her true feelings about Ana, but the whole affair seemed to have a celebratory feel to it.

"Well," Bailey said, making a pretense of rolling up her sleeves, "how shall we do this? Divide and conquer or stick together?"

Maddie gave her granddaughter a sideways glance. One day, she's gonna have to have a serious talk with that girl. "It's a big room," she said, "so why don't we split up and meet together after dinner to compare notes."

"Sounds like a plan," Bailey agreed, stretching her neck as if she was about to go into a fight. "Let's do this, Brutus," and she disappeared into the crowd.

Maddie took a much more calm approach to the task at hand. She remained at the entrance and carefully observed the crowd from a distance, hoping to find someone that would stand out. She let out a barely audible gasp as she noticed Chief Connors' Deputy Sheriff Fellows as part of the crowd. This was the second time she got the sense that Connors was doing more with the case than she had originally thought. She made her way over to him.

"Deputy Fellows," she said in greeting, "fancy meeting you here."

"Mrs. McDougal." He said, giving her a kindly nod. "Fancy meeting you here, too."

They stood side-by-side canvassing the crowd without speaking for a few minutes. Finally, Maddie couldn't resist any longer. "Deputy, I have to ask. Are you here on official duty or did you have a grudge against Ana, too?"

Fellows smiled at Maddie. "Boss told me you were the tenacious type," he said dodging the question.

"I think I just got my answer," Maddie said. "I think I'll just be moving along, I don't want to distract you from your work."

Maddie moved among the crowd listening to snatches of conversations as she passed by, hoping to glean enough information to join in on conversations about Ana so she could rule out suspects.

"She was no picnic to work with." She overheard Jessica's comment as she passed by. It was enough to make her stop.

"Jessica," Maddie interjected, "so good to see you again."

"Ah, Mrs. MacDouglas," Jessica smiled.

"McDougal dear," Maddie corrected, a little embarrassed as she eyed the people whose conversation she just interrupted, only to be called by the wrong name. She gave Jessica a chastising look that only a true Granny could pull off after being insulted in such a way.

"I'm sorry," she apologized. "I don't know what's wrong with my mind these days."

"There, there dear. It's probably just the stress of the last few days. It must be very hard at the office without Ana."

"Hmph," Jessica grunted. "We've never been happier. Ana was a nutcase if you want to know the truth."

"Really?" Maddie interrupted again. "How's that?"

A group sigh came in unison. "Obviously, you didn't know her very well," said a red haired lady that looked like a round butterball turkey.

"Anyone who had ever done business with her will tell you," a blonde woman with long, dangly nails joined in.

"Well, I was just about to get to know her when she passed," Maddie explained. "We were about to book a trip to Europe with her."

"Well, you should thank your lucky stars that you didn't," said a tall man with a Texas accent. "She probably would have charged you an arm and a leg..."

"And a foot."

"And an eye."

"And a kidney."

"And a..." There was a burst of laughter that ran through the group as they all enjoyed a little comic relief at Ana's expense.

"Wow! Tough crowd," Maddie joked.

"You won't find any Ana lovers here," one chubby little man said matter-of-factly. "Unless *you're* one of them."

"I have to be honest," Maddie said. "I'm a little lost right now. Since I didn't know Ms. Stevens, I simply don't have an opinion one way or the other."

"Well, what did you think this cruise was for? Didn't they tell you it was for all those who had a problem with Ana's business style? It's sort of to make amends for the wrongs she did."

"Well, not in so many words, but yes, they told me." Maddie agreed. "I just thought it would be more like a posthumous roast or something fun like that."

"Yeah, well. Wish we could have really given her a roast," another lady interjected. "On a spit that is."

Another burst of laughter from the group told Maddie that she was literally out of her league. These people were so angry about whatever happened that it would be difficult to narrow anyone down. And they were all outspoken.

She eased her way out of that conversation and moved through the crowd once again. She saw Bailey on the other side of the room, deep in conversation with a sharply dressed businesswoman. Maddie wondered whether she was getting anywhere with her conversation. She was pulled out of her thoughts of joining Bailey by a familiar sing-songy voice.

"Maddie, darling. I heard you had arrived," Thomas gave Maddie a gentle handshake, taking her hand and guiding her to a corner of the room where they could talk more privately. "I did a little legwork for you, I hope you don't mind."

"Oh, really? What's that?"

"Well, I knew that you didn't know all of these people so I kind of sorted them all out for you," he said. "Most of these people only have petty complaints against Ana. If you put them all together, they wouldn't even have enough leverage to make a decent lawsuit." He gave a nonchalant wave of his hand. "You don't want to bother with those. They'll be a waste of your time. What I did do though is put the heavy hitters at the same table with you for dinner tonight. That way, you'll get one-on-one time with each of them." He gave her a careful look like Astoria does when she's done something she feels she deserves a treat for.

Maddie was pleased. It meant that she didn't have to go on an endless fishing expedition looking for a virtual needle in a haystack. She rewarded him with a gentle grandmotherly type smile and a grateful thank you. It seemed sufficient, but she made a mental note to send Thomas a box of her famous cupcakes as soon as she was back at the bakery.

An hour later, dinner was announced and all the guests were ushered into an elaborately decorated dining hall. The room could have easily fed three hundred people at the ornately dressed tables, each capable of seating ten people around it. The round tables were laid out with what appeared to be some of the finest bone china she had ever seen and the silverware actually looked like real silver with gold trimming on it.

While Maddie was quite comfortable in the setting, Bailey tried not to look like she was never at such a posh affair, but it was hard to try to fit in when she looked down and saw three forks. She didn't know which one went with what. She felt the blood rush to her face, which apparently showed. With Maddie sitting on one side of her and Thomas on the other, she fingered her silverware trying to decide if she should wait until the food was served and then copy what the other guests were doing or just wing it.

Maddie however, leaned over to her and whispered. "Don't worry about the silverware darling. There's a simple trick that works every time. When the first course arrives, start with the first piece to your right, and work your way in from there."

Thomas, however, leaned in and explained the purpose for each of the utensils she had before her. Finally, he said, "Don't worry about it. Just follow my lead and you'll be just fine."

Maddie gave him a grateful nod. Now she knew she had to send him some cupcakes. He was a doll, but he was also a suspect so she needed to keep her wits about her for the time being. She muttered a quiet thank you and settled in for a lovely evening.

Next to Thomas was a couple; Parker Milhorn and her husband Andrew. Next to them was Michael Hale and his wife, Jessica and then Jessica, both employees of the travel agency. The last seat was a no show; Maddie decided she'd have to find out more about Janet Davis after the cruise.

By the time the first course had arrived, the wine had been flowing freely for quite a while and it took only a little prompting to get the tongues wagging and everyone in a relaxed mood. Thomas spoke first; as if on cue, he stood up and took a knife and hit the side of his glass. Maddie cringed at the sight. This was not just a regular glass from the kitchen; this was real crystal stemware. She hoped it would hold up to this kind of beating, but she was relieved when nothing happened. Thomas cleared his throat and waited for the room to quiet down.

"So, we know we're all here because we all knew Ana at some point in our lives and felt that she had in some way had an impact on us and our lives. Some of us have bigger stories to tell than others, but we at the

Stevens Travel Agency have scheduled this event in order to ensure that every one of you leaves here happier with our agency than when you came. Over the next few months, we'll be visiting each and every one of you in an effort to make amends for the losses or correct any issues that you may have experienced. In the meantime, enjoy your meals, and share some of your positive life with Ana stories among each other."

Parker, a tall, stately brunette in her thirties, with the air of an aristocrat was already a few shades into the wind. Her eyes had that slightly glazed look that gave you the impression that she was already impaired, but when she spoke, her voice came out in complete control.

"Let me start us off," she said. "My 'Life with Ana' story starts with our honeymoon. Oh, pardon me. I suppose I should introduce myself first." She placed her lavishly jeweled hand on her chest. "My name is Parker Milhorn and this is my husband, Andrew." The five-fingered jewelry case was extended towards a mousy looking little man next to her. "When we planned our honeymoon, we had made it very clear to Ana that we wanted a quiet little place where we could spend some time alone, just the two of us. Right honey?" She looked over at the mousy man next to her.

"Yes, dear."

"We were very adamant about that."

Maddie thought to herself that maybe Parker was adamant, but the man next to her didn't seem to know much about speaking up for himself.

"Anyway, Ana recommended a nice little Dude Ranch in Massachusetts. I thought it was a wonderful idea." Her hands were waving in the air with grand gestures for each sentence she made. "So we booked a week at the Tall Pines Ranch near Boston." Parker stopped to take a sip of her jostling drink she was waving around with her grandiose gestures.

Maddie thought she wouldn't make it to the end of the story and she was pretty positive that the drink wouldn't last whether Parker drank any of it or not.

Parker continued, "At first, everything seemed to be perfectly fine. We had a private room on the edge of the property, which was pretty well secluded from any of the other guests on the property. The first two days were fine. But then we got word that there was a blizzard coming. The hotel made us move from our private cabin and into the main quarters with the other guests." Parker stopped to take a bigger sip of her drink. This time she drained the glass. "Gan Bei!" she shouted.

Maddie's eyes went up inquisitively.

"Isn't that what the Chinese say when they finish a drink? Gan Bei?"

Weird, Maddie thought.

"It means, dry the glass," Parker added, proud that she had added a little bit of trivia to offer the group. "Any way," she continued, "that wouldn't have been so bad, but we later found out that we couldn't even get a private room during the storm, which lasted for two whole days. They had the nerve to make us share a bunkhouse with twelve boy scouts. Now, how is that for a honeymoon story?" She finished nodding her head as if everyone was in total agreement with her. "I ask you," she added, "wouldn't you have been furious? I mean, they could've at least comped us for a couple of free days or something after that."

Maddie wanted to say something to the effect that the place had no control over the weather or the conditions after the storm hit, but she knew that Parker was not in the mood to entertain the possibility of anyone defending Ana at the time.

"And to top it off," Parker continued, "the next three days were spent cleaning up from the storm. We had no electricity, no running water, and no privacy."

During the entire time, her mousy husband Andrew never made any comment. He just sat quietly by and listened while his wife relayed the story that he must've heard hundreds of times by now.

Parker finally regained her composure. "So that's my 'Life With Ana' story."

Maddie just looked at the woman. She didn't know what to say that would possibly make her feel better. She began to believe that the idea of having an Ana bashing party was not as therapeutic as many people may have thought it would be.

Silence fell around the table for a moment while people, apparently feeling uncomfortable after the story, tried to decide what to say. Thomas stepped in and had the DJ play some music so he could regroup.

Maddie pulled the couple aside to a smaller, more private table to let them finish the story to her and Bailey. Parker continued, "We tried to sue, but our lawyers said we didn't have any case. They said that neither the travel agency was negligent nor the ranch. Since they had no control over the things that happened, there was nothing they could do." Parker's anger was beginning to get riled up again. "I'll tell you what they could have done," she said, the anger building with each word as she slammed her jeweled fists on the table. "They could have given us our money back or at least given us a free vacation package or something." She leaned across the table and eyed Maddie. "You know what we got?" she asked. "You know what we got? Nothing. Not even an I'm-sorry-we-ruined-the-most-important-week-of-your-life."

To everyone's relief, the waiter passing by with an overloaded tray of dishes broke her emotional outburst. A sign of relief went around the table while the dishes were served. After the waiter had moved on to another table, Parker remained silent and the rest of the guests at the table breathed a sigh of relief.

For a few minutes everyone ate in relative silence, while listening to the music, which turned out to be a little less awkward as Parker's trip to the past.

Chapter Five

The dinner had turned out to be a great success; the guests were now content and enjoying their complimentary cocktails while strolling around the deck of the beautiful boat. The night was perfectly clear so they could bask in the moonlight and stargaze until time to retire.

The conversation had moved from Ana to other sordid stories that turned out to be infinitely more entertaining. After all, how long did it take to rehash unpleasant experiences from the past? Especially after the person no longer has a voice of her own. Madeline walked in silence, taking in the crisp, clear air, the first in weeks since the rains started. It was refreshing to be able to relax for a moment.

But her respite was short lived. Thomas rounded the corner, obviously in search of more gossip to spread. He seemed to relish the chance to get in on a little juicy chatter about Ana. "Maddie," he breathlessly exclaimed, "I finally found you." She was leaning on the railing, deep in thought. "I've searched the boat from top to bottom looking for you." He gave her a playful little tap on the shoulder. "Why'd you disappear like that?"

"I just needed a little time to process my thoughts."

"Well, I suppose you do. It's a lot of information to process in one evening, don't you think?" He leaned up against the ship's railing, mirroring Maddie's position. "I knew that there were plenty of people that were upset with Ana, but I didn't know to what extent."

"I find that really odd that you would say that Thomas," Maddie said, eyeing the tattler. "I mean, weren't you her assistant? It would seem to me that you would know just about everything she was doing."

"True, true," he agreed, "but she didn't tell me every single thing she did. And I wasn't with her so long that I knew about all those people and how they felt."

"Oh really? How long were you with her?"

"Only about three years. She had a real problem letting me take on more responsibility in the company. She said I gave them a bad image." He folded his arms in front of him and stood as if he was about to ward off a defensive attack.

"Wow, that must have really bothered you."

"Yes, it did. I mean I really know this business, but she wouldn't let me do anything but push papers around." He waited a minute before he continued, "Well, the joke's on her because now I'm in charge of the whole office."

"Well, you certainly seem to know what you're doing, Thomas."

"If you give me a chance, I can turn any business around. I understand business management, accounting, travel, and everything you can think of to deal with the industry. But all Ana could see was the outer shell and she couldn't get past that."

"Well, Thomas, I can tell that you have your finger on the pulse of this business. As a matter of fact, I'd really like to shadow you and follow you around to see if you could teach me a few things about how to get more efficiency out of my own business."

Thomas appeared genuinely flattered by Maddie's suggestion. His Cheshire cat smile reminded her of Astoria, who wasn't allowed to take the trip with her. "Why of course! I'd love to show you the ropes," he answered, pride oozing from his voice. Extending his elbow, Maddie gladly accepted it and together they walked from the deck to the lounge area.

"Isn't it kind of late for more activities?" Maddie asked. It seemed that most of the guests were already heading to their cabins for the night.

"Of course, but we need to make arrangements for tomorrow night. We have a host of events going on throughout the day and I have to make sure every detail is exactly right."

She watched as Thomas made his way from one area of the boat to the next, deftly taking care of every minute detail of each event scheduled. She allowed him to ramble on casually while she took in everything he had to say about Ana. It wasn't long before she was able to glean that he didn't appreciate or value his boss in any way. Thomas was excruciatingly honest in his appraisal of her and he made no pretense of trying to be nice about it.

It seemed to be par for the course for the evening. It was the way everyone seemed to feel about her. Maddie wondered just how much more about Ana she didn't know.

"So, Thomas," she started, "it's no secret that you didn't care for Ana very much."

"No, I didn't," he agreed.

"So, why did you stay with her? Couldn't you have found a job at another agency?"

"Well, I certainly thought about it. But, I was indebted to the company because they sponsored my education. I did my internship under Ana and she offered me the position afterwards. Besides that," he added, "Rockcrest Cove is a very small town without a lot of opportunity for an aspiring travel agent."

"So, why do you think she didn't want you to move up in the company? It sounded like she invested quite a bit in your future."

Thomas was silent for a minute while he mulled over her question. "Like I said before, she said that I would be a pretty bad image for the company. She had a major issue with my lifestyle choices, if you know what I mean."

"I do," Maddie said, "but didn't she know that about you before? It couldn't have been news to her."

Thomas looked surprised at Maddie's conclusion. It was true. Ana had known about his lifestyle before he began working for her. There had to have been another reason why she didn't want him to move up in the company. "Well, I guess it just meant that she wanted to be at the top all by herself, I suppose."

You could hear the anger and frustration begin to rise in his voice. He tried to change the subject. "So, what have you found out from all those people you talked to tonight? Did you learn anything that stood out as suspicious?"

"A few things, but I'm just not ready to talk about it right now."

"Oh, well that's a disappointment. I'd really like to know where your investigation is heading."

"Well, Thomas. I do want to thank you for all the help you've given me. I wouldn't have been able to narrow it down without that list you gave me."

Thomas became serious for a moment. "I guess what I'm asking is if you have anyone that you're considering a real suspect yet."

Thomas was certainly not what Maddie had expected when she started investigating this case. She studied him for a moment, trying to figure out if he would be honored or mortified by the prospect that he was being considered as a suspect or not.

"Well, I'll tell you this much. You're certainly on my list of people who didn't like Ana, but not liking someone doesn't naturally make one a murderer."

"That's nothing. Everybody on this boat, with the exception of you and your granddaughter, have the same feelings."

"Some stronger than others," Maddie agreed. "But you...your feelings are different."

Thomas turned his attention away while he fiddled with a flower arrangement on a center table. "How so?"

"Well, most of the people here have lost money because of poor business dealings. But they had a choice to go to another agency or go online when they wanted another vacation. But you...you have been tied to Ana for your entire professional career. She sponsored your education, gave you your internship, and you helped her build up her business over the years with no reward for your hard work. As a matter of fact, it sounds like she was actively trying to keep you from becoming a full participating member of the business." Maddie paused before she made her next statement, "It almost seems like she had something over you that compelled you to remain in her employ as a lower level member of the business." She paused again, "Was Ana blackmailing you for something?"

Thomas froze in his position for just a moment. He didn't respond nor did he direct his attention to Maddie in response. Finally he said, "Don't be silly. What could she possibly have to blackmail me on?"

"Thomas." Maddie said calmly, "Did you have any reason to kill Ana?"

"Well, I can't say I didn't think about it once or twice," he answered with trepidation in his voice and continued, "but I didn't kill her. I'm just not that kind of person. I couldn't possibly do something like that."

Maddie studied the young man and she decided that she honestly believed he didn't kill Ana, but she had a strong feeling that there was still something more to the man standing in front of her. She made a mental note to discuss it with Bailey when she got back to the room.

The day's activities were quickly winding down and Maddie was feeling a bit exhausted from the events of the night before and being Thomas' shadow as he sailed from one task to the other. She excused herself and decided to take a break on deck with a Mimosa after brunch. She was perfectly content to sit and watch the comings and goings of the many Ana haters and observe them without their knowing. Although she was already beginning to formulate an idea of who the killer was, she was convinced that he or she was on the boat and that she would have solved the crime before they docked once again.

Chapter Six

The following morning Madeline and Bailey had just about had enough. They wanted at least one day when they didn't have to hear people rant about their issues with Ana. It was painfully obvious that the woman had little regard for anyone other than herself. Exhausted, they both plopped down into two lounge chairs and settled in for a little R&R.

Maddie wore her big sunglasses so that people would not realize that she was observing them and Bailey was sporting a cute little spaghetti strap coral sundress with a matching headband. Her sunglasses weren't as obvious as Maddie's, but they did the trick. They knew that as long as people thought they were just unwinding and enjoying the sunshine, they were more inclined to act themselves.

The only problem, Maddie thought, was that no one seemed inhibited about talking about Ana. She'd never heard of someone having so many enemies.

While she had already ruled out quite a few people, there were still a few that were clearly at the top of her list.

While she was meditating on all those who were possible suspects, figuring out the angles and motives for each one, a young man arrived and, without saying a single word, fell into the lounge chair next to them. An exhausted sigh escaped his lips and both women gave him a surprised look that he didn't seem to notice.

"So," Maddie said, breaking the silence. "Mr.???"

"Hale. I'm Michael Hale," he said as if she should already know who he was. "Don't you remember me from the dinner last night?"

"Oh, yes. Mr. Hale." She did finally recognize him. "I'm so sorry, but yesterday was kind of like a whirlwind." She gave him a warm smile and put a gentle hand on his and he seemed to calm down. She said looking in the direction of Mr. Hale. "Do you have an Ana story you'd like to share?"

Mr. Hale had the appearance of a powerful businessman dressed in his full-blown business attire. Maddie gave him a visual appraisal and wondered what was his story. He wore a three-piece, finely tailored business suit. Who wears a business suit on a Paddleboat Cruise, she wondered. He seemed extremely uncomfortable with the crowd and looked out of place. He looked a lot like Mr. Bartlett Finchley on that episode of the Twilight Zone where the machines all turned on him.

He carefully folded his hands together before he started by addressing the story Parker had told the night before. "I can certainly relate to Mrs. Milhorn's tales of woe on her honeymoon. It was unfortunate indeed that she would have had such a horrid experience. However, I must congratulate her on leaving well enough alone after that awful first experience." He placed a hand on his chest and continued in a slight British accent, "I on the other hand, did not have the common sense to take my business elsewhere and as a result have had the misfortune of being taken by Ana on two separate occasions."

Both Maddie and Bailey sat up in their lounges to give him their full attention. They leaned in to hear the details of Mr. Hale's 'Ana experience.'

"On the first occasion," he started, "I invested several thousand dollars into an Egyptian Archeological dig. We were to explore the sight of the lost city of Tanis for six weeks. My wife and I were thrilled at the prospect. Unfortunately, we arrived in Egypt only to be told that the entire excursion was cancelled due to a sandstorm in the region." He paused for effect. "We were given one free night in a 5-star hotel and then sent home." He gave a long sigh of exasperation, "And I had donated nearly $20,000 for the privilege."

The ladies both gave a surprised gasp to reward him for his story so far.

"When I approached Ana about a refund, she told me that because my payment was considered a donation and not an actual fee for the trip, there was nothing she could do. The money was already sent to the archeological team that was sponsoring the dig."

Speechless, Maddie couldn't think of any way she would have recovered from a $20,000 loss. As a matter of fact, she couldn't even imagine having $20,000 to spare for a single vacation. "And what happened the second time?" she inquired.

Mr. Hale looked as if he had completely forgotten that he had said two experiences to tell, but he quickly recovered. "The second event was even worse. This time, I made sure that the money I gave was not a 'donation.'" He made the air quotes sign for donation. "But again, the trip was cancelled."

"Another sandstorm?" Parker asked, obviously intrigued by the man's money.

"No, worse," Hale answered. "This time it was government intervention. It appears the Egyptian government was not inclined to have foreigners digging around their historical sites, something about the possible removal of ancient artifacts from the country. They cancelled my visa and sent me back home on the next flight. I didn't even get the free hotel night that time."

Hale let out a final breath of air to indicate that he had finished his story and there were no more details to add. He finally turned to the two women with a look of expectation. "Well then?" he said as if expecting something for his troubles.

Maddie and Bailey looked at each other, confused. "Well what?" Bailey responded. She was getting a bit tired of the "my tragedy is worse than yours" attitude. It seemed that everyone was trying to one-up each other in an attempt to sell the saddest story.

"What's your Ana story?" Hale finally asked.

"Oh," Maddie said. It hadn't occurred to her that everyone would be expecting her to tell her own tale of woes in exchange for their revelations.

"Well, my story is not nearly as engaging as yours," she said, trying to think fast and come up with a believable story. "We booked a cruise, much like this one," she said, "and the cabins were absolutely horrible." She continued, "They were in such poor condition, we were forced to get off at the first port, and fly home. The toilets were backed up, the air conditioner didn't work, and there was an awful stench in the air."

"Oh my," Michel responded. "Well, I hear there's a rumor going around that she didn't have an accident like they said." His eyes studied the two women to make sure that he had their full attention. "They said that she was murdered." He said the sentence very slowly to give the right effect.

"Oh my!" Bailey said, feigning intrigue.

"Well, if you ask me, it's good riddance. The woman created nothing but pain and misery for nearly everyone she met." Michael stood up, adjusted his tie and was off to his next story telling experience without so much as a goodbye.

The two watched him leave and Bailey cried out in exasperation, "Gran, I can't take this anymore. Is it possible for one person to be hated so much?" She started rubbing her head as she stood up. "I'm going back to the cabin for a little bit of peace and quiet. If I hear one more Ana story, I'm gonna scream."

"Maybe we should head back to the cabin. I'm pretty sure that we're getting close to identifying the murderer. I'm positive they're on this boat with us."

"Are you sure Gran? There are plenty more people that belong to the "Hate Ana" club that couldn't make this cruise."

"There's no doubt about that, but from some of the things I've heard, if anyone hated her enough to kill her, they'd make sure that they were on this boat."

~~~

Back in the cabin, Bailey kicked off her shoes and fell down on the bed. "Gran, who do you think it is?" she asked with her face in the pillow, her voice muffled.

"I have my suspicions, but I haven't decided yet."

"I think it's Thomas," Bailey announced.

"Granted, he is high on my list Bailey. But I'm not so sure."

"Why not?"

"First, remember our first clue. The earring. And second, he just doesn't seem like the type. I don't know. My gut tells me that it's not him. But I do think he knows more than he's sharing."

"Like what?"

"I'm not sure. He's giving the appearance of being supportive, but he's holding back," she said, thinking out loud. "I think Ana was blackmailing him or holding some secret over his head. Why else would he choose to stay in such a horrible working situation?"

"Good point," Bailey agreed, "But my money is on Hale. That was quite a story he had to tell."

"I know, but he's a man of pretty good means. $20,000 is a drop in the bucket for him. For someone to want to kill, losing money has to hurt. He seems to be just inconvenienced. Did you see that suit he was wearing? It probably cost more than $20,000 all by itself!"

Bailey was deep in thought considering their options. "Well, we need a little more information about Ana. There's a lot more than meets the eye. We should call Eleanor. See what's she's come up with while we've been away."

"Good point," Maddie agreed. "Did you bring your cell?"

~~~

Eleanor answered on the first ring. "My goodness, I was beginning to wonder if you two had forgotten about me? What took you so long to call?"

"Oh, Ellie. We've been so busy here. It's just one thing going on right after another."

"Well, I hope you have some information for me, I mean you've been there for three whole days."

"Yep. Two more to go," Bailey groaned. "Not what I was expecting for a Paddleboat Cruise."

"Did you find out anything interesting?"

"Sure did," Maddie said, "a lot."

"I did, too." Eleanor said. "Wait until you hear this." The two women leaned into the phone to hear the details. They thought about putting her on speaker, but decided against it just in case someone may have been listening at the door.

"Your Police Chief friend, Connors, has decided that Ana's death was not an accident after all."

"Really?"

"I don't know what happened, but he's actually launching his own investigation into Ana's death."

"The travel agency has been shut down pending an investigation of the entire staff."

"Oh my goodness! They must've uncovered something that we don't know about."

"Well, according to a friend of mine at the Coroner's office, drugs were found in Ana's blood stream. The amount of drugs found in her blood could have been the reason she fell down the steps."

Maddie and Bailey looked at each other. This was certainly a new twist in the case. "Or pushed," Bailey added.

"Evidently, they feel that it was not enough to kill her, so they think that she was drugged just enough to get her disoriented and then hit on the head with something. Then the murderer staged the fall to cover it up."

"So, the true murderer would have some access to drugs of some kind."

The three women shared notes and discussed the details of the case well into the evening. By the time they hung up the phone, Maddie was pretty sure that she knew who the killer was, but she needed one more piece of evidence to cinch it.

Chapter Seven

The final night of the cruise promised to be the most exciting of the entire week. A formal dance affair had everyone arriving at the ballroom in his or her most elegant clothes. By the end of the five-day cruise, it seemed that most of the guests had also tired of the Ana bashing and had moved on to other subjects.

The room had been elaborately decorated to represent a trip around the world with each service station featuring cuisine from that region. The ballroom was adorned with decorations from each of the seven continents lined the walls surrounding the dance floor in the center.

Maddie and Bailey had arrived early so they could choose a table in the front of the room near the dance floor allowing them to see everything that was going on. Back in their room, they had decided to dance with as many of the men as possible and buddy up with many women to see if they could determine the killer before the night was over. They were both mentally and physically exhausted from the all-inclusive cruise and were looking forward to the entire thing being over with soon.

The room was in full swing with a live band playing to a latest collection of tunes from around the world and everyone was having a great time. Bailey was being swung around the dance floor by a middle-aged man, Paul, who was filling her ear with his story of a botched African safari and Maddie was resting her aching feet while chatting away with Parker at their table. An involuntary yawn escaped her lips as she sat through another long version of the same story of their ruined honeymoon at the dude ranch. She was quite thankful when Thomas, turning out to be an insightful man, extended a hand and pulled her up on the dance floor. As much pain as her feet were in, she still welcomed the chance to get away from Parker and enjoy herself for a minute.

As they spun around the floor, Maddie was quite surprised that Thomas had turned out to be such a good dancer. Interestingly enough, he also proved to be adept at maneuvering the conversation back to where he wanted to go. She sensed that he was more serious than ever and she began to worry that he had become more concerned about him being named as a suspect.

"So, have you discovered the identity of the elusive killer?" Thomas asked.

"I've narrowed it down to a number of primary suspects," Maddie answered. "And I have you to thank for that."

"Moi?" He feigned surprise, but for once Maddie wasn't entirely sold on his act.

"Yes, you," she confirmed.

"But, I told you. I'm just not that kind of person. I couldn't possibly kill a fly."

Maddie gave him a genuine smile. "Oh, but Thomas, I think you can kill a fly if he was annoying enough. But, while you may be at the top of my list, there are a few other suspects that I still haven't ruled out yet."

She was a little surprised to feel the tension in his muscles relax in response to her words and realized that while he put on the pretense of having everything under control, the death of his employer had really worried him. She bit her lip and contemplated this man she was getting to know quite well.

"Well, who do *you* think it is?" she asked him.

Thomas took a step backward, raised his arm, and spun her around before he answered. "Well," he said thoughtfully, "Michael Hale had a pretty compelling story, don't you think?"

"Well, anything is possible, I guess," she contemplated all the information she had collected so far and said, "but there is still a lot to be considered and any one of these people could be the one."

"But look at all the money he lost at the hands of Ana," he stated. "If you ask me, he's probably lost more money than all the people here combined."

"Perhaps, but money is not the only motivator for murder."

Thomas was quiet for a minute. "I suppose, but it would be a big one for me," he conceded.

Maddie eyed him suspiciously. He seemed to be pushing Michael in her direction for some reason. Thomas spun her around the room once again, sending her into a bit of confusion for a minute.

"You know," he thought aloud after a rather elaborate twirl. "If you hadn't delivered your specialty cookies when you did, it's no telling when Ana's body would have been found."

Maddie stopped for a brief second and eyed him more closely. How did he know that I was delivering cookies to Ana? She thought about all of the conversations she had had with Thomas since that awful day and was quite sure that she had never told him anything about what was being delivered. She also thought about the muddy footprints that were leading away from the back door. It has been raining all night; certainly they would have been washed away before she arrived that morning. That meant that someone had to have been at the house that day or had only recently left. So many things were running through her mind at the time that she felt she needed a break.

Maddie stared at Thomas through a new lens. Here was a man that appeared to have it all together, but something was off. She couldn't quite put her finger on it, but Thomas was not turning out to be who he appeared to be.

Thomas' face reddened under her scrutiny and he took a self-conscious step backward. "Um, I'm afraid you'll have to excuse me," he said finally, "I have to check on the menu in the kitchen." He turned and left Maddie standing alone on the dance floor.

She stared after him and then slowly walked back to her table, deep in thought. She had only sat at her table for a few seconds before Bailey was at her side.

"Gran, what's wrong?"

Maddie didn't respond.

"Gran, I saw what happened. What's wrong?"

"Oh, Bailey," she said, snapping out of her revelry. "It's Thomas. I'm rethinking what I had originally believed about him."

"I know, Granny. But what did he say?"

"Nothing major, honey. He just asked me about the cookies I delivered for Ana." She said thoughtfully.

"Well, chances are he's her assistant so he probably placed the order for her."

"I don't think so. This was for a private event, not done through the agency. I'm sure I didn't tell him about the cookies." Maddie was trying to remember that first conversation with him. "I'm sure I told him about the delivery, but not about the cookies." She said finally, "I never reveal the contents of any of my customers orders for events. It's a policy I've always had."

"So, how did he know?" Bailey questioned.

"I don't know, but I will find out!" Maddie said, thinking out loud.

Bailey looked around the room of characters. All of them had a reason to hate Ana, but she felt that the majority of them just disliked the lady. And most of them didn't dislike her enough to want her dead. Those that ranked at the top of her list still didn't give her enough evidence to prove that they were the killer. Something was missing. She turned back to her Gran. "Listen, Gran. I think we need to go and have another chat with Eleanor. We're missing something."

"Good idea. Maybe she can fill in the blanks for us." But Maddie didn't move.

"What's wrong Gran?"

"I'm thinking that the only way Thomas would have known about the cookies was if he was at the house when I delivered them."

"Yeah, but Ana died the night before, right?"

"Mmm hmm. That's right."

"So maybe he arrived after the murder just like you did," Bailey reasoned.

"Possibly, but when I was at the house, no one was there. I left after the police arrived so he couldn't have been hiding somewhere. The police would've found him. He must've been there before I arrived. The footprints could have been his."

"Let's go back to the room and think this thing through. This way we can run it all by Eleanor and see what we can come up with."

Chapter Eight

Bailey turned around in the small cabin. She was trying to pace, but it wasn't very effective considering the room was only large enough to allow for three or four steps before she had to turn again. She liked to pace when she was in deep thought, but this was proving impossible. She plopped down on the bed instead.

"Ok, what have we learned about Ana?" Maddie started.

"We learned that we were lucky to have never met her," Bailey said. "I've never seen someone with so many enemies."

Maddie gave a slight chuckle. "You're absolutely right, but let's review the details anyway, shall we?"

"Sure, good idea," Eleanor's voice came over the speaker on the laptop Bailey had brought with her.

"All right, let's see," Bailey started, "she's the owner of the most exclusive travel agency in town."

The other two agreed. "What about competition?"

"She has no competition—it's the only travel agency in town."

"But has she made it impossible to start a new one?"

Maddie sat upright in her seated position. "That's an angle we've never considered."

"What's that?"

"Thomas. He's certainly capable of opening up his own agency and yet he chose to be in a lesser position and work for Ana. That always felt wrong to me."

"Do you think Thomas had to get rid of Ana in order to take over the agency?"

"Well, he certainly had his finger on the numbers of everyone who hated Ana. He didn't have to look very far to find out what we needed. Maybe it's something he's been planning all along."

"That's true," Eleanor agreed. "It was almost as if he was expecting someone to come investigate."

"He certainly did seem prepared," Bailey added, "and this cruise. It's hard to believe he could pull something like this together in just a matter of a few days."

"But it still doesn't quite feel right. He just doesn't strike me as the murdering type."

"Well, let's put him aside for the moment. Who else do we have?" came from the computer.

"We have Michael Hale," Bailey put in.

"Who's that?"

"He's the one that lost thousands of dollars on two failed archaeological trips. Ana wouldn't give him a refund," Bailey contributed.

"That could prove to be a strong motive," Eleanor said pensively.

"Yes, but those trips were years ago. Why would he wait until now?" Maddie asked. "Besides, Eleanor, if you could see him you'd know $20,000 is nothing to this man. He'd hardly notice it missing."

"Still, he's worth considering. He's still angry enough to come on this cruise and vent his feelings about Ana," Eleanor added. "Once you've been burned, it can sometimes be hard to forget. I know I've seen plenty of people kill for far less than that."

"All right," Maddie complied, "that's suspect number two. What did you find on your end?"

"Well, you two have found tons of Ana's enemies, but I've found just the opposite. She has loads of people that absolutely adore her, including the mayor and his wife."

"Really?" Both Madeline and Bailey seemed surprised.

"From your perspective it may seem like everyone in the world hates the woman, but I can assure you that's not the case. As a matter of fact, it was the mayor's wife that pressured Chief Connors to start the investigation of her murder."

"That's it!" Maddie exclaimed. "I knew the old crank wasn't smart enough to figure this out on his own. Someone had to be behind him starting the investigation."

"Well, you're certainly right on that account," Eleanor agreed, "and there's another thing you were right about. While she has plenty of friends that are willing to step up to the plate and support her, she still has her share of enemies as well." Eleanor began shuffling through a stack of papers on her desk. "Bailey your computer skills paid off. Hacking into her email account brought up loads of useful information. It is loaded with emails from people who hated her completely. Some of these emails can actually be considered threatening by today's legal standards."

"Yeah, Bailey is really good at chopping computers and getting information for me," Maddie said proudly.

Bailey fell back on the bed, rolling her eyes, "It's called 'hacking' Gran, not chopping."

"Oh, sorry, Bailey," Maddie apologized. "I don't think I'll ever get the terminology just right. Bailey is good at hacking," she repeated to Eleanor.

"Well, that package you sent me took me a while to go through, but in it I found hundreds of threatening letters, emails, and texts in her personal files."

"Wow!"

"But when I went online, I found a host of angry reviews about her travel agency. It's obvious she has more than her share of unsatisfied customers. I'm willing to bet that the majority of them are right there on the boat with you."

"When you were going through them, Eleanor. Did any one of them stand out as being more threatening that others?"

"Quite a few actually." Eleanor commented as she looked carefully through the papers. "You have to be pretty angry to write threatening comments to someone and send it through the Internet. Anyone who does that must have lost all manner of reason. They must know that it will eventually be brought to light."

"Well, that certainly makes sense for a logical thinking person, but some of these people here have been burned two or three different times. And with Ana having the only travel agency in town, if you wanted to book a nice excursion, you had to either handle all of the details yourself or travel to the next town to find a service to do that."

"Good point. So, the concept of free enterprise was lost. These people were forced to work with Ana on such specialized travel packages so she repeatedly ripped them off because there was nowhere else they could go," Bailey started to reason.

"Eleanor," Maddie declared, "I need to see those emails you found. I think if we had them here Bailey and I could compare them to our notes on the people we've met on the cruise and come up with a viable suspect to hand over to the deputy sheriff here."

"There's a deputy sheriff on board?"

"Yes, I thought that was strange and I couldn't figure out why until you told me that Connors has decided to investigate the case himself."

"Well, he may very well come in handy. It sounds like you're getting close to finding the killer. You want to stick close to him so that you're not in any danger darling."

"Point well taken," Maddie conceded. "So, can you go through some of those papers and pick out ones that you really feel stand out from the rest and send them to me on my E-phone?"

Bailey sat bolt upright in the bed, nearly bumping her head on the upper bunk above. "It's I-Phone Gran. It's an I-Phone, not E-phone. It stands for Internet Gran, get it?"

"Oh." Maddie turned back to the computer. "Can you send them to my I-Phone?" She asked looking to Bailey for her nod of approval.

Bailey gave her a thumbs-up sign, but it looked like her Gran was never going to get this new lingo even though she tries so hard. A look of pity, frustration, and sorrow fleeted across her face as she contemplated a future of explaining new terminology for the next twenty years.

"Also, can you go to my office at the bakery and find the notes I wrote on Thomas Jones and send them to me as well? There's something about him that isn't adding up and I want to look more closely at my first impressions of the man."

"Why, is he a primary suspect?"

"Absolutely. He certainly has the motive and I believe that Ana may have been blackmailing him for something, but I can't get him to really open up."

"You will," Eleanor encouraged. "You will. You have that way about you that makes everyone want to open up to you. Just be yourself and they'll tell you everything you want to know."

"I hope you're right, Ellie," Maddie said exasperated. "But we've still got a little bit more digging before we can root out the killer. Right now there are too many possibilities; we need to narrow it down even further."

"You're right," Eleanor agreed. "Can I make a suggestion?"

"I'm open."

"Why don't you get with the Captain and the deputy sheriff and give them a list of your top suspects. Then have them all invited to a private room for cocktails, that way you can scrutinize them without distraction from the other guests on the boat."

"That's an excellent idea!" Bailey said. "We've already ruled most of them out anyway."

"I wish I was there with you!" Eleanor whined.

"You are," Maddie encouraged. "You are with us, but Ellie, I think there's just one more thing I'm gonna need you to send me."

"Sure thing sweetie. What's that?"

"The picture of the earring that we found on the bottom of my shoe. Can you send that to me as well?"

"Sure thing. I'm going to send them all to your I-Phone like you wanted, but I'll also fax them to the Captain's cabin, too. That way you can print them out and have a hard copy to work with."

"Sounds like a good idea." Maddie took a deep breath, "Well, here goes. By this time tomorrow, we'll be back home with the case closed—we hope."

Chapter Nine

The small room off the Captain's quarters was a welcome relief for Maddie and Bailey both. It was a quaint little private dining room the Captain often used to entertain his more elite guests when on the water, though only large enough to hold a group of about ten people comfortably.

The Captain stood by the doorway to greet his guests in his official uniform—a black, well-fitted captain's jacket with the four epaulettes on the shoulders and a snappy captain's hat held securely under his arm. His curiosity was definitely piqued as he stood at the door awaiting his guests.

Maddie had approached him to tell him her plan. Captain Evans had reservations about the whole affair, but was definitely intrigued by this tiny woman attempting to solve a murder on her own. He agreed to the private party on the condition that he have his own ship security in the room with the suspects, who would only be informed of their role in the fiasco after they'd arrived.

She had arrived earlier that evening to make sure that everything was ready. A folder with all the information she needed was tucked safely away behind the bar and she was quite sure that the killer would reveal him or herself long before it was needed, but it was always safe to have a good back up plan. Deputy Sheriff Fellows was to be her escort for this small and intimate cocktail party and the only ones that knew what was to happen was the Captain, the deputy, Bailey, and herself. Even then she felt a little uncomfortable, but the Captain insisted it had to be that way. The only thing she could do was comply with his orders.

As expected, Thomas was the first to arrive. He appeared a little miffed that he was not allowed to have a hand in planning this intimate affair. After all, it was his travel agency that had booked the cruise and he felt slighted that the Captain would call a private affair without consulting with him first. He wore a nicely tailored navy blue leisure suit that was far removed from his usual flamboyant style of dress. It gave off a very professional image that spoke of his newfound position in the company. Bailey entered with her hand on his arm, working hard to reveal her mortification at being escorted by the likes of Thomas. But as usual, she would always be willing to comply with her Gran's wishes, no matter how strange.

Captain Evans greeted them warmly and handed them over to a hostess to show them their assigned seat at the table. Bailey immediately sat down in her seat when the waiter pulled her chair out for her, but Thomas remained standing.

"Thank you," he told the waiter when his seat was indicated, "but I need to check on the events of the evening to make sure they go right."

"I appreciate your dedication to your job," the deputy commented, "but for this event, you're not working. Why don't you sit down and act like a real guest for a change?"

Thomas' face was full of insult, but he took his seat just the same, perching himself right on the edge. Resting his chin in his hands it was obvious that he didn't know what to do when he wasn't working. He took his assigned seat next to Bailey and started fiddling with the napkins on the table.

"You don't know how to be normal, do you?" Bailey asked.

"Pardon?"

"You don't know how to be just a normal guy. Sit down. Have a casual conversation. You have to be right in the middle of everything, don't you?"

"Well, I'll have you know that I'm plenty normal."

Bailey gave him a small smile that showed her irritation was fading. In its place she felt a little pity for him.

Maddie came and joined them at the table, taking a seat next to Thomas. As usual, she was perfectly perched to see everything going on in the room. Not that it mattered; the room was small enough that nothing would be done without being observed by others around them. "What a lovely evening," Maddie started. "Wasn't it nice of the captain to have this little private soiree for us?"

"Yes, I suppose so," Thomas said peeved. "I just don't understand why I wasn't informed about it."

"Well, there's always a reason for some things Thomas, even if we don't understand them at the moment," Maddie gave him her most grandmotherly type voice.

There was movement near the doorway and they looked up to see Michael and his wife make their appearance. Clearly, they wanted to be recognized as the wealthiest of couples on the boat, which wouldn't have taken too much effort. Their grand appearance was greeted with gasps as Mrs. Hale entered dressed to the nines. Maddie thought that they had gone a little overboard, but she guessed that a personal invitation from the Captain can do that to some people.

Maddie could tell from the scornful look on his face that he was disappointed to see the rest of them there. He actually thought he was going to be spending an evening with an elite class of people. She chuckled a little within herself, but she only allowed Michael to see her most sincere face.

The Milhorns arrived shortly afterwards. Parker was again jeweled to the max, with diamonds and gold dripping off every finger and dangling earrings. It occurred to Maddie that she might have been the one that lost the earring at Ana's house. She would have to find a way to work that into the evening.

Eleanor had arranged to have everything Maddie had requested couriered to her by powerboat. Paddleboat cruises were not meant to take passengers far or fast so a powerboat could easily have caught up with the lumbering boat as it meandered gracefully in the river.

There is only one person missing, Maddie thought and as soon as she arrived, the show was ready to start. She didn't have to wait long for Jessica to appear at the door. She seemed winded and flustered as she stumbled into the room. Then Maddie realized why—she had been drinking, and quite a lot by the looks of it. She wondered why she and Thomas had not arrived together. A quick glance at Thomas told her that they had a falling out of some sort. The two cut eyes at each other and it was apparent to everyone that there was no love lost between them. Once Jessica was seated at the table, Maddie gave the Captain a nod, he gestured to his security team and they took their position at the door.

Maddie stood up at the table and looked at the group in front of her. One of these people was a murderer and now was the time to prove it. She cleared her throat and started.

"First of all, I want to thank all of you for coming to this small event on such short notice." She glanced around the table and saw confusion on everyone's faces with the exception of Bailey, who knew what was about to happen.

"I need to explain something to you. The Captain extended each of you an invitation at my behest. This event was planned by me, not the Captain."

"Well, that explains it," came a snide remark from Thomas. "Had I known, I would have been more than happy to offer you some assistance in planning it." He cast a negative glance at the meager dinner table decorations.

"You're probably right, Thomas. I've spent a few days with you by now and I know that you are the best when it comes to planning a party."

Thomas seemed to be a little appeased by the compliment, but still not quite satisfied at being excluded.

"At any rate, I've asked you all here to help me to solve the case of Ana's murder."

"Murder!" Parker exclaimed. "I thought it was an accident." She looked genuinely surprised.

"That was the police's initial ruling," Maddie concurred, "but recent discoveries have indicated that there was enough evidence to arouse suspicion of foul play." The table was silent as they all looked up expectantly waiting for more news. "And I believe, that the murderer is right here at this table with us today."

There was a cacophony of chatter that erupted at the audacity of the statement. Maddie continued, "I will show you my evidence and then explain to you why I think you may have had the motive and the opportunity to commit such a heinous crime."

She began to pace around the small room as she spoke. "I have to confess to you that I have never met Ana, nor have I done any business with the woman."

"What's that story you told me about...."

Maddie raised her hand to stop him in midsentence. "I'm sure that some of you believed that I was here to vent my anger the same as you and I allowed you to believe that so that you would speak to me freely as you already have done." She canvassed the table and saw offended looks, but not outright hostility. "So, shall we begin?"

The Captain reached under the bar and brought out the evidence folder and handed it to her.

"My involvement with this case started a little over a week ago when I arrived at Ana's home to deliver an order of baked goods for a private party she was planning for the evening. I found the door to her home open and on closer inspection I found this scene in her kitchen."

She laid a photo in the center of the table and everyone leaned over to get a closer look.

"As you can see, the table is set for two people, but only Ana's body was found. The spilled wine had been there long enough for it to dry and leave the wood flooring stained, probably permanently. This indicates that the murder had happened the night before and the culprit had long left the scene."

The group remained speechless, attentive to her every word. "But what was most interesting was this." She pulled out the earring and showed it to the group. "Naturally, when I discovered this little piece of evidence stuck to the bottom of my shoe, I assumed that the killer was a woman." She placed the earring on the table so that everyone could see it. "But when it arrived here on the boat by courier last night, I noticed something different. Notice the post there? It's rather thick for an earring. Most earrings actually have a thinner post so that it can go through the ear without having to apply a lot of pressure, but this post is nearly double the thickness of an average earring."

The men at the table leaned in a little closer to examine the object. They had not paid much attention to women's earrings before, but this actually intrigued them a little bit. Parker actually took one of her earrings off and laid it next to the object and they could all see that it was indeed considerably thicker than an earring post.

"That lead me to one conclusion. It's not an earring at all, it's a cuff link, and that would naturally belong to a man."

"Are you saying that the killer is a man at this table?" the Captain asked.

"No," Maddie said. "What I am saying is that a man at this table can actually identify the murderer because he was there the night Ana was killed."

Murmuring broke out around the table. "Well who is it?"

"Don't keep us in suspense!"

"So, I got to wondering, what person knows the most about Ana and all of the things she's done? Well, when I asked that question, only one name came to mind. Thomas Jones."

"Ahhhhh," Thomas jumped from his seat shrieking like a little girl. "No!" He cried running towards the door where the Captain's guards deftly blocked his way. He turned back to the crowd. "I didn't kill her. I didn't. I swear!" He pleaded with the group. He knelt down in front of the guards and began to bawl loudly. "I'm not a murderer, I'm not."

Maddie toyed with him for a moment and then calmly stated, "Of course, you didn't Thomas."

Everyone in the group turned and looked at Maddie confused.

"But you just said..."

Maddie raised her hand again to stop the chatter. "I know. I understand the confusion, but if you'll just bear with me one minute, I'll explain." She paused to wait for the chatter to die down.

"At first, Thomas was very high on my list of suspects. He had the most to gain from Ana's death. He was second in command; he would finally get the recognition and the bump in salary that he felt he deserved. She had kept him in the shadows for years, which certainly gave him the motive." She paused to catch her breath. "And he knew about the order being delivered to her house. My guess is he probably frequently visited her house to discuss company business."

"That's right," Jessica pointed out. "At least twice a week."

"But why did you rule him out?" Parker asked.

"It wasn't until last night that I realized who the real murderer was." She started walking around the table, speaking to each individual in turn as she passed. "The proof came in the package with the cuff link. My friend went online and looked at reviews about the Stevens Travel Agency. There were many complaints posted there, but several were extremely bitter and harsh." She pulled out a paper from the folder. Here is the proof of the real murderer." She gazed over at Thomas. "Care to tell us who it is?"

Thomas looked up, his face streaked with tears. "It was Jessica!" he shouted, pointing an accusing finger in her direction.

"What!?" Jessica appeared shocked at the accusation.

Everyone in the room seemed totally taken aback that innocent and quiet Jessica could have actually been the murderer. "How did you surmise that?" Maddie asked.

"You're right," he said. "I did know about the order because I had been with Ana the night before." He started to wipe his tears. "We always met together throughout the week and Ana always loved your cookies. She would actually have me come and pick them up for her, but that night I was busy, so she called to have them delivered."

He paused for a brief moment and looked at Maddie. "Anyway, we were talking about a problem with Jessica always getting the customer's information wrong. Ana said that this was part of the problem with a lot of the customer complaints. So, she asked me if I thought we should get rid of her."

"So, you were planning to fire Jessica?"

"No. No, we were just talking about it. Nothing had been decided yet."

"So, then what happened?"

"Well, we didn't know what to do so we simply decided to leave it be for a while. We went on to some other business matters and just before I was to leave, the doorbell rang." He started to sob again. "It was Jessica."

They had to wait until he got his composure together again. "Anyway, it looked like she had been drinking and I tried to talk her into going home, but she wouldn't." He looked up at Maddie. "I didn't know what she was going to do, I swear." He started to fiddle with his fingers.

"The next morning I had a bad feeling about that night so I went back to the house to check on Ana. I tried to reach her by phone, but I got her voicemail." He paused to get his emotions in check and to try to stop the flood of tears that were flowing again. "I had a spare key to the house, so I let myself in. That's why the door was ajar when you arrived," he said to Maddie. "When I heard you at the front door I was afraid that you would blame me for what had happened so I ran out the back door and hid behind the cottage."

"But you didn't tell the police?" Michael Hale asked.

"No. The police said it was an accident so I didn't say anything."

"When did you realize it was Jessica and that she had murdered Ana?" questioned Maddie.

"Well, right after her death I received an email from one of the business review sites with a complaint about Ana. The email was anonymous, but it was obviously written by someone inside the company because they knew details that the average person didn't know."

"But that meant it could've been anyone who worked there."

"Not exactly," Thomas corrected. "This person had inside knowledge about salaries, personnel contacts, even business dealings that the average employee in the front room wouldn't know. They even had contacts overseas that others wouldn't have even known existed. That narrowed it down to only three or four people."

"So, how did you narrow it down to the one person?" Maddie asked.

"Well, if I had to guess, you have the same email in your hand right now. And the answer is in the subject line."

Maddie laid the paper down on the table and everyone leaned forward and read the subject line, "To the End of Anna's Reign."

Michael looked confused. "I don't see what's wrong with that line."

"I do," Maddie said, and so did Thomas. "Ana's name is spelled with only one 'n', not two."

"Well, people make spelling mistakes all the time," Michael commented.

"But remember, this is a person who has worked alongside Ana every day for years. Who do we all know that is notorious for getting names spelled wrong? How many of you have had to correct Jessica on the spelling of your name more than once?"

Everyone's hands slowly went up in the air. Jessica jumped from her seat and fled to the open doorway. As the guards were busy holding onto Thomas, she was able to slip by them and down the hallway. One guard went after her, while the other one still held a firm grasp on Thomas.

"So, congratulations Thomas, you were the first one to figure it out. I just have one question. Why didn't you report her to the police when you realized it was her?"

"I thought I could use it to my advantage. So many people hated Ana, I didn't think anyone would care if she was gone, but I figured that if there any attempt to move Jessica into place ahead of me, that I could use that as leverage so that I would be pretty much guaranteed the top job. Jessica could be my assistant."

The guard came running back into the room, "She..." he panted, "she...she jumped overboard."

"That's all right," the Captain spoke. "I alerted the Coast Guard and they are waiting offshore to pick up any possible runaways."

The ship's guards pulled Thomas up to his feet. "Don't worry about this one Captain. We'll keep him in holding until we dock and the local police come and collect him."

As Thomas was being pulled away, his wails could be heard all through the deck. People in their cabins were all coming out to look and see what was happening.

~~~

Once the two were removed, a round of applause broke out around the room. "That was very impressive," Michael complimented her.

"I cannot believe you solved it," Parker said. "You certainly had me fooled."

"That was the plan," Maddie explained.

The Captain encouraged everyone to drink and enjoy the rest of the evening while he went to his office to report the latest events. When he returned, he pulled Maddie aside.

"I feel it is only fair to warn you."

"Me?"

"When you get off this boat, there will be a lot of press there asking you questions."

"Really? It's not me they should be talking to."

"Well, they seem to want to ask you for more details about the..." he stopped to refer to a paper in his hands. "An Emma Larson case? They said you solved that crime, too."

"But that was almost a year ago. They should have forgotten about that now."

"Whatever the case, you did a splendid job here and I hope there is a reward for your dedication to bringing justice back to the community."

Epilogue

One Week Later

The bakery was in full swing. Once again, the news had traveled fast and spread throughout Rockcrest Cove like a windstorm. Everyone had been talking about how the case with Ana had been solved by the mild-mannered bakery woman downtown. People were coming in by the dozens to buy her goods and deliveries were becoming more of a mainstay than she had originally thought.

By afternoon, everything had begun to settle down and Maddie had a chance to sit back and catch her breath. Just before closing though the doorbells chimed announcing one more customer. She almost got up to check it out, but she thought better of it. *The girls could handle it*, so she let it go.

But soon after, Rachel came to the office. "Ms. Maddie, you have a visitor."

Maddie sat up in her chair and pushed her glasses up on her nose. "Who is it?"

"It's Captain Evans," Rachel replied and ushered him in.

Maddie stared at the gentleman and hardly recognized him wearing street clothes. "Thank you Rachel," she said as she saw the young girl mouthing the word "cute" behind the captain's back. She gave Maddie the OK sign and a thumbs-up before she left the room, closing the door behind her.

"Captain," Maddie said, standing up and offering her hand.

"I'm not on duty now. You can just call me Phil."

"All right, Phil. What brings you here this afternoon?"

"Well, I have to be honest," he said, a little embarrassed. "I don't usually do this, but I thought that I might come by to take you to dinner."

"Dinner!" Maddie looked surprised.

"You do eat, don't you?"

Maddie felt a little bit flustered. "Of course, I eat," she answered.

"Well then, I thought that if you eat and I like to eat, that tonight, we might be able to eat at the same place at the same time. What do you think? Your girls said that you were just about to close."

Maddie gave him a genuine smile. "I think I'd like that, but I have to stop off at home first." She pointed to her canvas bag. "I have to drop off Astoria."

Astoria peeped her snow white, pearly head out of the bag. She had long been ready to leave the bakery and go home.

"That's fine with me," Phil said.

"Just let me change my shoes," she said and sat down behind her desk. The familiar vibration of her phone told her that Bailey was calling. She held up one finger. "Excuse me," she said and pulled her cellphone out of her back pocket.

"Hey Gran, are you about finished with work?"

"Yeah, we're closing now."

"I thought I'd drop by and we can go take in a movie or something."

"Oh, I can't tonight dear. I've got plans."

"You've got plans? You never have plans."

"Well, I do tonight. How about I call you tomorrow and we plan on something together?"

Bailey was dumbfounded. Her Gran had never had anything to do but work and spend time with Astoria, now she had plans? She hung up the phone and looked at her watch. "Now, what was she going to do?"

<u>Coffee, Tea, Murder:</u>

A city council party catered by local pastry chef Madeline McDougal suddenly goes dead... LITERALLY!

A fun event quickly takes a turn for the worst when one of the town councilman in attendance, Kipper Rio, is discovered dead. With no solid leads to go on as to the perpetrator of the crime, and the local police chief way out of his league. It's now up to Madeline with the help of her friends, to do some "snooping" and expose the killer.

If this murder case is going to get solved, Madeline and the gang need to move quickly and quietly. Unsavory characters are all players in this "deadly game," and the guilty party won't hesitate to kill again in order to protect their dark secret.

Find out what Maddie discovers in book three of The Rockcrest Cove Mysteries! Get Your Copy Today!